We
Belong

We Belong

COOKIE HIPONIA EVERMAN

ILLUSTRATIONS BY ABIGAIL DELA CRUZ

Dial Books for Young Readers

DIAL BOOKS FOR YOUNG READERS
An imprint of Penguin Random House LLC, New York

First published in the United States of America by Dial Books for Young Readers,
an imprint of Penguin Random House LLC, 2021

Text copyright © 2021 by Cookie Hiponia Everman
Illustrations copyright © 2021 by Abigail Dela Cruz

Visit us online at penguinrandomhouse.com.

Library of Congress Cataloging-in-Publication Data
Names: Everman, Cookie Hiponia, author. | Dela Cruz, Abigail, illustrator.
Title: We belong / Cookie Hiponia Everman ; illustrations by Abigail Dela Cruz.
Description: New York : Dial Books for Young Readers, 2021. | Audience: Ages 10 and up. |
Audience: Grades 4–6. | Summary: Through a bedtime story to her daughters, a woman weaves
together her immigration story and Pilipino mythology. Includes glossary, songs, and author's note.
Identifiers: LCCN 2020047593 (print) | LCCN 2020047594 (ebook) |
ISBN 9780593112205 (hardcover) | ISBN 9780593112212 (ebook)
Subjects: CYAC: Novels in verse. | Mothers and daughters—Fiction. | Sisters—Fiction. |
Immigrants—Fiction. | Folklore—Philippines—Fiction. | Philippino Americans—Fiction. |
Philippines—Fiction. Classification: LCC PZ7.5.E94 We 2021 (print) | LCC PZ7.5.E94 (ebook) |
DDC [Fic]—dc23

Printed in the United States of America

10 9 8 7 6 5 4 3 2 1

Design by Cerise Steel
Text set in Granjon LT

For Diana, my moonbeam
For Tala, my starshine
Every story is for you, my hearts

For Marishka in the Morning.
Thank you for everything.
Heartcha always.

Mama, tell us a story

For as long as I can remember,
children in my family have asked this
of every mother in my family.

"Mama, tell us a story."

Tonight, as they do every night,
my children ask it of me.

Some mothers, daughters, and sisters
sew, paint, or cook their stories;
my mothers and I sing ours.

Mama, tell us a story.

Sure, Stella, just a sec, okay?
Luna. Hey Luna moonbeam,
have you brushed your teeth?

I did, Mama.

You always say cleanliness is next to godliness,
and my teeth are next to godliness.

Mmm. Minty godliness.
Okay, no more comics.
Lights down. Let's get tucked in.

Aw! Just one more p—

Luna.

Fiiine.

Thank you.

Mama, a story? Please?

First let's make sure
you have everything you need
for your field trip tomorrow.

Daddy already signed
the permission slip last week.
I just need to bring a sack lunch.

Remember to put on plenty of sunscreen
and wear your hat the whole time.

Ugh, I hate sticky sunscreen!
Won't I just get super brown and look like you?

Absolutely not. You're pale like Daddy, and
he gets freckles just going up the driveway for the mail.
Without sunscreen, you'll get crispy like lechón!

Maamaa! Don't bite my arm!

Then wear sunscreen!

Okay already! Now a story!

Story! Story! Story! Story! Story!

All right, all right! Sheesh!
What story do you want to hear, my hearts?

Shall I tell you the one about
the moon, the sun, and the star?

Or shall I tell you the one about
the poet, her brother, and her sister?

No, Mama. Tell us your story.

Every story I tell you is my story, anak.

Tonight, I will tell you
Mayari's heavenly family story,
the story of outsiders
who had to work four times harder
than everyone else to inherit the Kingdom of Heaven.

It is very like my family's story, our own mythology.

So tonight, I will also tell you
my Aguila family story,
the story of immigrants
who had to work four times harder
than everyone else to dream the American dream.

When I hear Mayari's story, it is like listening to my own,
like reading a story that anyone who looks like me
knows by heart. Mayari and I share a name—

Wait. Mama, your name is Elsie, not Mayari.

Just as my story is not exactly like Mayari's story,
my name is not exactly like Mayari's name,
but we share our one true name: Buan.

I don't get it. That's your middle name, not your real name.

Oh, my heart, what's real is not always what's true.
Buan made it her life's work to reflect light;
I think it must be my life's work to reflect love.

You see, a great love is like a light
that shines through in loves that come after.
It is reflected in the great love

between me and my sister,
between the two of you,
between all sisters.

And my first story begins with that great love,
between Mayari and her sister, Tala.

I will tell you their story as Mayari would tell it,
from the beginning of everything.

Little Star

When my sister, Tala, was born,
my heart found its other half.
"My baby," I said, reaching for her hand
and gently rocking her cradle.

"Could you sing my lullaby to her, sinag? Mayari?"
asked my mother, who was cleaning after dinner.
We were all drowsy, getting ready for bedtime.
I sang to my baby the lullaby that Nanay had been
singing to me forever.

Kislap, kislap bituin
Ano bang 'yong gawain

Sa ibabaw ng mundo
Parang hiyas na bato

Kislap, kislap bituin
Ano bang 'yong gawain

Tala has been my dearest love for lifetimes.
I have loved others, reached for other lights in the
darkness, but none compare to my little star.

Tala . . . *TA-laaah*

my sweetest
my brightest

my heart
my song

the bridge between our big brother and me,
between day and night, between light and dark.

Between worlds
there twinkles a little star.

Tala . . . *TA-laaah*

A Simple Kind of Life

My days took shape around making Tala's eyes sparkle,
making her wonder at the magic of stones and leaves.
It was my job to keep Tala happy
while my family worked

and I was so good at it, her whole face shone
when she smiled.
She sang before she talked; danced before she walked.
We grew in those fields together,
sun-kissed and content.

Every morning at dawn,
our family would go out to the fields:
Tatay carrying his bolo over his shoulder,
Nanay carrying Tala liwanag, our starshine,
Kuya Apolaki, our eldest, carrying our lunch basket.

All I carried were the flowers I picked,
the stones and feathers I gathered,
the songs in my heart,
all of it for Tala.

Kuya would lay out our banig
under the shade of a langka tree.
Nanay would place Tala on it,
smile at her and kiss her head.
Tatay would ruffle my hair and
tickle Tala until she giggled,
then the three of them would walk off
into the rows of crops nearby.

I taught Tala the name of
every plant around our little house
the way Nanay taught me and Kuya.

Nanay sang the world to life for us,
starting with a song describing our bahay kubo—
our palm hut—surrounded by Earth's bounty.

Bahay kubo, kahit munti
ang halaman doon ay sari-sari

Singkamas at talong, sigarilyas at mani
Sitaw, bataw, patani

Kundol, patola, upo't kalabasa
At saka meron pang labanos mustasa

Sibuyas, kamatis, bawang at luya
Sa paligid-ligid nito'y panay na linga

When the sun was highest in the sky,
Tatay, Nanay, and Kuya would come back to our banig
with fresh fruit to go with our lunch.

Nanay would take Tala onto her lap
to snuggle and nurse.
Tatay would lay out our meal leftovers
wrapped in banana leaves.

Kuya and I would eat our lunch quickly
so we could play.

Sometimes we would stay close to the banig,
pick up branches and play-fight,
pretending to be warriors.
Tatay would laugh and show us
how to hold our sticks properly.
Tala would stop nursing and clap in delight.

Sometimes we would go to where Tatay set up the traps
to catch tikling birds so they wouldn't eat our crops.
We would imitate how the birds dodged the bamboo
sticks, stepping in, out, through, like graceful dancers.

Much too soon, we would stop what we were doing
to rest our bodies while the sun did its hardest work.
Tala would already be asleep in Tatay's arms.
Nanay would call me and Kuya back to the banig.

We would race to reach her and throw our arms around
her waist. She'd plant a kiss atop each of our heads and say,

"Amoy araw kayo."
"You smell like the sun,"

like sweat and dirt,
like laughter and childhood.

When the sun started its climb back down to earth,
I would look across the horizon, over the fields, and see
Tatay, Nanay, and Kuya walking toward us
with the vegetables we would cook for dinner.

Tala would ask for someone new to pick her up,
her chubby fingers reaching toward the purpling sky
while I gathered our things to put into the basket
so Kuya could roll up the banig to carry it home.

We walked back to our bahay kubo,
retracing the morning's steps,

stopping by the river to wash off the day's toil,
splash away the lingering heat on our skin,
get fresh water,
maybe catch a fish or two if we got lucky.

Our evening meal, like lunch, was often
just vegetables and rice,
flavored with what little meat or fish
we could get that day,
but Nanay made everything taste like food for the gods.
Tatay would rub his belly and exclaim, "Sarap!"

After dinner, Nanay and I cleaned up
while Tala swung in her duyan.
Tatay and Kuya rolled out the banig and spread out
cotton blankets on top, making a comfortable place
for us to sleep, side by side, in our one-room hut.

Nanay would take Tala out of her cradle
so she could nurse for bedtime.

Then Nanay would sing us all to sleep,
as she did every night.

It was a small life, but it was our life.
We found magical beauty in the ordinary.

And we were happy.

But as in all faerie tales, we would learn
all magic comes with a price.

Sunrise, Sunset

The days of our life were long,
but the years would be short.

Our mother's years—how could we know?—
were getting shorter and shorter.

One long day, Nanay could not get out of bed.
She was counting out her last breaths,
like she used to sort stones from grains of rice . . .

In the suffocating silence, our mother called out,
"Bathala!"

"She must be dying," said Kuya, tears at his eyes.
"She calls for God."

"She calls for me," Tatay said. "I am Bathala."
He knelt by her side and took her hand in his.

On that long day, our parents told us
who we truly were, what life we had lived.

"You are the children of Heaven," Tatay said,
"but you are also the children of Earth

"made of starlight, laughter, sweat, and dirt;
made of the love between two people
from different worlds."

It was sunset on the last day of that life.
There was time for nothing else but truth.

"I am your father," Tatay said, "but also
the father of all. I am Bathala Maykapal.

"People call my name when they need to feel safe,
when they feel lost.

"When I fell in love with your mother,
I decided to live on Earth,

to live a human life of ordinary magic
not found in Heaven."

Nanay may have sung the world to life for us, but
Tatay had created the world for her to sing about.

"And it was your mother's song," Tatay continued,
"that drew me to the river on the day we met . . ."

Full of Grace

On the day he met the love of his life—
"Nineteen short years ago today," Tatay recalled,
smiling weakly at Nanay, his dying beloved—

Bathala Maykapal, Great Creator God,
was walking around the world of his creation
disguised as a humble water buffalo bull.

I.

Bathala the kalabaw was splashing,
happy in a mud puddle, when he heard singing.
It was soft and sad, but hopeful.

He ambled toward the sweet song
and discovered a maiden in the river,
surrounded by the inky darkness of her hair.

She was as lovely as her voice,
so lovely that upon seeing her,
Bathala the bull gasped, a sound so human

that the maiden looked up, startled, afraid,
and froze at the sight of the carabao,
a gentle beast, but a beast nonetheless.

Bathala felt shame and guilt
for disturbing her peaceful bath,
for making her afraid of him, of what he might do.

Bathala the bull turned around,
walked back into the forest,
and disappeared into thin air, leaving Earth.

The following day, he returned,
this time in his human form,
to seek the maiden at the river.

Bathala the bull must have really scared her, for
she did not return to the river that day, nor the next.
Bathala the man returned every day, hopeful, humbled.

On the seventh day, his heart soared when he saw her
walking toward the river with other women from the
village, carrying full baskets of clothing to be washed.

"K-kumusta?" he greeted her quietly
once he had caught up to her.
She turned her head in his direction and nodded silently.
"Mabigat ba 'yan?" he asked, hoping
she'd agree it was heavy.

In answer, she handed him the basket
and smiled, cheeks pink,
which emboldened Bathala
enough to ask her name.
"Dalisay," she replied,
tucking a strand of hair behind her ear.

Dalisay . . . *DA-lee-sigh*

Dalisay. Pure. Perfect.
It was the most beautiful sound he'd ever heard.
"Dalisay," he said softly. It was almost like praying.

II.

The days of their life together were long,
full of ordinary beauty and a love that kept growing,
even after so many years.

Theirs was a great love built of a thousand tiny touches.

One of my earliest memories, out in the fields:
Tatay dipped his cup into the bucket of fresh water
and offered it to Nanay first, making her smile.

Nanay touched Tatay's cheek, making him smile back.

Nanay took the cup from him and took a small sip,
then turned the cup a half-turn and offered it back
to Tatay, who drank without taking his eyes off
his beloved.

A smile shared. A moment. It was like watching
a red hibiscus bloom.

As they both began to look older,
Nanay would pluck the gray hairs out of Tatay's ears
and trim his bushy eyebrows, teasing him,
"What sorcery, gray hair!
Makes you look older but more handsome."

Did she allow his sorcery, his deception?
Did she know then that he was God?

On the long day of our mother's death,
our father brought his beloved a bowl of chicken broth
and held it gently to her lips so she could take a small sip.

A drop of blood escaped from Nanay's mouth,
a bloom of red death.

Tatay wiped her mouth with a clean rag,
cradling her head.
All day long he had insisted on staying at her side
and caring for her, leaving us, their children,
to fetch, cook, clean, worry.

Outside, night was drawing the curtains closed
so we could say goodbye.

The Long Goodbye

"Dalisay," Tatay said softly, "mahal ko,
it is time for me to take you home."

"I am already home," Nanay said,
smiling weakly at Tatay, her beloved.
"You must take them. Take your children."

Kuya Apolaki, Tala, and I were no longer children,
but we did not know how to be anywhere
other than where we were, touching Earth,
singing of what we saw and had in our mother's world.

Nanay asked for us to gather around her, then,
and she gently laid a hand on each of our cheeks in turn,

tracing her fingers over our faces like she used to do
to calm us when we were babies,
now for the last time.

"Your hair has really grown out," Nanay said to me,
smiling as she brushed my long hair away from my eyes,
tucking the strands behind my ear, lovingly, deliberately.

Her eyes were clear for the first time in weeks;
her gaze burned.
She called me her "beam of light" so I would heed her.
"Listen well, Mayari sinag. Watch over them.
All of them."

"Nanay," I whispered, "huwag po.
Please don't send us away."
I clutched her hand to my face, desperate to hold on,
and she tried to pull it away, gently first, then firmly.

"Tama na!" she rasped. A sputtering cough,
a red bloom.
"Your father will look after you now;
he will give you a home.
You must go.
Take your rightful place at his side."

I shook my head and begged her for more time.
Weeping, desperate, I snatched at her hand again.
"Nanay! Please!"
She snatched her hand back and slapped my face.
"I said 'Enough!'

"That will sting long after I am dead," she spat out,
the last bit of fire in her body sparking in her eyes.
Then those embers went cold, and she turned her back.

"Leave me."

Mama, why are you so quiet?

Mama. Are you okay?

I'm okay, Luna. I just . . . I just remembered . . . something . . .

How could she send her kids away like that?
You said she sang to them and loved them.

So how could she hurt Mayari and order her to leave?
Mayari must have thought, "You're not my mother."

Only bad mothers hurt their kids.
Only a bad mother would do what Dalisay did.
Right, Mama? Mama?

Mama, why aren't you saying anything?

Sometimes even good people, good mothers,
do things they never thought they could do
because they're worried, because they're scared.

Sometimes even good people, good mothers,
get so scared, they forget who they're supposed to be.

Why I Was So Quiet

I couldn't tell Stella and Luna why.
Best I could do was remember.
For me then, for all of us now.

They say having a child
is like having your heart
walk around outside your body.

They also say
your heart is a muscle
the size of your fist.

I am four years old
when my mother teaches me this,
when she shows me that her heart
is not only the size but also
the shape of a fist.

And her heart beats outside her body.

I shouldn't have
walked home from preschool
with a new friend
instead of waiting for Kuya Nes.

I shouldn't have
gone over to my friend's house,
just across the street, to play
with her dolls from Hong Kong.

I shouldn't have
made excuses for
my stupidity
my ignorance
my forgetfulness.

My heart beats with a rhythm of regret.

Shouldn't have.
Thump thump.
Shouldn't have.
Thump thump.
Shouldn't have.

But she can't hear the beating of my heart.
She is preparing me for the beating of my life.
She once sang me lullabies; now she hisses my name.

"*Elsaleta.* How could you do this to me?"

My mother orders me to strip off my uniform.
My heart beats faster, louder.
I feel it will burst through my thin kamiseta.

So sorry.
Thump thump.
So confused.
Thump thump.
So scared.

My mother wraps her fist with my father's leather belt
like she is Muhammad Ali before the Thrilla in Manila.

Snap! I claw the floor, and I am thankful
it's not the brass belt buckle striking my flesh.

Snap! I keep crawling, but her reach is long,
aided by my father's complicit leather silence.

Snap! I finally manage to crawl into a corner
and put my arms over my head.

She throws aside the belt
and makes her hand
into the shape of a heart.

Her fists beat
my arms,
my shoulders,
my exposed legs.

Then she drags me from my corner
and beats on my back, like it is a drum.

I hear someone sobbing.
Maybe it is me.

When it is over, my mother has to go lie down.

My grandmother comes downstairs from her apartment,
wraps a towel around me without looking at my face.
It is a yellow towel dotted with tiny baby-blue flowers.

Lola Lusing silently
dries my sweat,
wipes my blood,
tends my wounds.

The next time I see my mother,
I don't recognize the darkness in her eyes.

Gone is the woman I called Mommy,
who sang the world to life for me,
whose heart was not shaped like a fist.

This woman who woke from her nap
is all sharp edges,
hard to wrap my arms around.

I do anyway, even as I think,
"You are not my mother."

My mother would have
been just as worried and angry,
but she could not have done this to me.

My mother would have
chosen to teach me
how to protect myself from harm
instead of teaching me
I had to protect myself from her.

My mother would have
sounded more convincing
when she said "I am sorry."

I search for my mother, still. Not
the mother of my birth, but
the mother of my heart,
the mother of my longing-to-belong heart,
the mother who would make me feel safe enough
to be in the world.

I search for her in the story of Dalisay,
mother of three demigods,
who drove her child Mayari away
as any mother would have
if she thought she could save her daughter
from death and human pain.

I search for her in every mother in books
and TV and movies and games.

I'm disappointed to find the same mother,
who doesn't make me feel safe,
who doesn't make me feel accepted,
who doesn't make me feel I belong.

Mama, you're still very quiet

I'm just thinking about the next part of the story,
when Apolaki, Mayari, and Tala had to leave their
home on earth.

Mayari must have been so scared when Dalisay
sent them away.

Well, thankfully, Mayari had Tala to keep her
from being too scared.

Mayari sure loved Tala a lot. She said Tala was her baby.

Hey, you call Tita Tala your baby, too, Mama.

Yes, your auntie was my first baby.
Tita Tala is like every Tala,
like all the stars in our stories: warm and radiant.

Tala was the brightest light in Mayari's life.
Tala was Mayari's sister and best friend.

They were a team! Like me and Ate Luna.
We're Team Miller.

That's right, starshine! And just like Team Miller,
Mayari and Tala carried each other.

Just like your Tita Tala and I carry each other.
Sometimes I think she is stronger than I am.

Elsie's Tala

When my sister Tala was born, my heart
found its other half.
"My baby," I said, my hand on the hospital window.
Even then I reached for her light, her warmth, her hope.

Tala began saving me when she was only three years old,
when my mom gave my dad the responsibility of
disciplining our bodies.

It was after Mom had finished beating on her heart,
after Lola Lusing had gone back upstairs,
after my own heart had begun scabbing over
in order to protect itself.

Kuya Nes and I had torn down Mom's curtains,
swinging on them like Tarzan.

This show of rebellious freedom required
Dad's leather justice.

Ever-efficient, Dad had us both kneel
by the big bed, bums facing out.
Tala, who had never gotten in trouble,
wandered onto the scene.

"I want to play this game, too!" she said brightly.
A smile.
She kneeled next to me by the big bed and said,
"Ready!"
Dumbfounded, Kuya and I looked at her, then at
our father.

Dad's mouth had fallen open.
We braced ourselves for what was next.

To everyone's surprise, including Dad's,
what came next was laughter.

Tala's superpower, then and now:
Shine a gentle light on what is happening.
"Ay sige na nga," Dad relents. We freeze. Could it be?
"Go on! Get out!"

Tala, disappointed, said, "That wasn't a very fun game."
More laughter.

That night, Kuya and I both gave Tala our dessert,
a meager thanks, as it turns out.
Our father never again hit us with his leather belt.
Outside, the frogs were singing their evening song:
kokak, kokak, kokak.

Mayari's Tala

Our mother, Dalisay,
was the second-most important light
in the sky of my life,
a light that was dying fast.

After she slapped my face,
I left our bahay kubo and ran
down to the flower garden.
I needed to look upon all the beauty
that Nanay could make with her hands.

For an hour, I cried in the garden,
my heart heavy with the dark hurt
of being rejected by someone you love.

When I saw a torchlight approaching,
I knew for certain it was my baby, my star.

Tala smiled at me, though her eyes were puffy.
She lit the lantern in the garden, then sat next to me,
and took my hand in hers, holding both in her lap.

"Ate Ari, your kare-kare was delicious,"
Tala said. "It tastes just like Nanay makes,
but I think Tatay just wasn't very hungry tonight."

I wiped my face with my free hand and turned to her.
"I'm glad I'll still be able to make it for you when—"

I turned away from her then, unable to finish my sentence.
I took both my hands and put them to my face,
wet with tears.
"Nanay didn't mean to hurt you," Tala said quietly.

"I . . . I know . . ." I said, now taking Tala's hand in mine.
"Nanay called me Mayari sinag like she used to . . ."
My tears were hot.
Tala liwanag kissed my hand, our silent way
to say "I love you."

We sat like that together for a long time, listening
to each other breathing,
to the world getting ready for bed,
to the winds whistling through the trees,
to the frogs singing.

Sometimes when I hear the frogs now,
I remember that night in the garden,

where two sisters wished
for a happier ending

just like in so many faerie tales,
where magic frogs speak and grant wishes.
I listen, hopeful, but still all I hear is *kokak*.

Motherless Exiles

Our mother had returned to the earth
from whence she came.
Our father had gone back to his kingdom in the sky.

Our world had at once grown to include Heaven and
shrunk to the circle of earth between the three of us,
huddled beneath the langka tree
under which a banig and a basket of food
were all we needed,
under which our mother was now buried.

We watered the ground with tears we had saved
when we could cry only for ourselves and each other.

"Tatay has given us seven days to decide: stay or go,"
Kuya said, solemn.
"If we go, we are to take only what we can carry."

The three of us sat silently for a moment,
thinking about the weight of everything
that we could not take with us to our father's kingdom.
I wanted to take these fields, this tree, our home,
the flowers I had picked since childhood,
the feathers I had gathered to tickle a baby Tala,
the sound of Tatay and Kuya play-fighting with sticks,
the smell of Nanay's kare-kare . . .

Tala reached for Apolaki's hand,
then reached for mine. She beamed.
"Our songs are light; we can always carry them,"
she reminded us, diamonds in her eyes.

That night, we packed a banig for each of us,
a bit of dried fish and rice, some clothes . . .
how many shirts and malong does one need in Heaven?

The next day, we met our sister Bighari for the first time
at her rainbow bridge to the sky, her bahaghari,

to join our father's other children who were whole
gods (not half, like us),
to see our father in his true form—
no gray hairs or bushy eyebrows—
where we were welcomed not
with open arms but secret whispers,
where we would have to prove we belonged.

All we had now were each other, our songs,
and our names: Apolaki, Mayari, Tala.
We were motherless exiles, wretched refuse.

Bighari

Bighari was the youngest child of Bathala,
the last one born before Bathala met our nanay.
Bighari was a child of Heaven,
but she was happiest on Earth.

Bighari so loved Earth, she often disappeared
into the wilds of our father's earthly kingdom,
playing in fields where wildflowers grew,
weaving blooms into crowns and necklaces.

Bighari so loved playing among Earth's flowers,
she once failed to show up for a family meeting.
Her siblings pleaded with Bathala to give her a chance,
but: "If she loves it so much, she can stay on Earth forever."

Little did Bathala know that he, too, would one day
want to stay on Earth forever, would want long days

and long years, would want to see
red bloom for love, not death.
But at that moment, all Bathala knew was
Bighari's disobedience.

Later that day, Bathala's messenger came down to Earth
to find Bighari and banish her on behalf of our father.
"Bakit?" she asked, in tears. "Why can't I come home?"
"I am sorry, miss. I am only the messenger."

Bighari, motherless exile, wretched refuse, wept bitterly
for hours, until the sun rose. She wiped her tears and
thought about what came next.
At first she thought of appealing to Bathala,
but she knew it would be fruitless.
Our father could be stubborn.

She decided to make herself at home
exactly where she was.

Bighari, artist, scientist, created
thousands of new flower varieties,
with colors and scents
nobody on Earth could have imagined.

Then, one day, she began weaving a bower
over her beloved garden:
a giant arch of red, orange, yellow, green,
blue, indigo, and violet blooms.

Bathala looked down from his heavenly kingdom
and saw what Bighari had done.
Awed and humbled, Bathala softened his heart
toward his daughter,
who was building a bridge to the sky,
up to Heaven, back to him.
At once Bathala sent his messenger to fetch Bighari
and bring her home.

On the day we met Bighari for the first time at her
bahaghari, our sister wore a crown of flowers,
her purple malong pinned at her shoulder.

She hugged each of us in turn, her long-lost siblings.
"I am so happy to meet you all!" she gushed.

While we ascended, Bighari talked to us
about what to expect in Heaven:
"It is basically Earth, but you can't die." A laugh.
"Well . . ." A long pause. "You *can* die . . .
if too many people or gods forget your name,
if too many no longer call for you in prayer."

Bighari must have seen the alarm on our faces.
"Oh, don't worry. Bathala would never let anything
happen to you. Our father has spent the last few weeks
talking about you to anyone who would listen."
A smile. "Everybody knows your names."

The golden gates of Heaven opened
with Bighari's gentlest touch, and
Bathala's messenger bowed before us,
then took us to our father.

Bathala, resplendent in a malong woven of starlight,
opened his arms to welcome us to his kingdom.
"My children!" he cried, beaming.

That night, at our welcome banquet,
we sat at the head of our father's table,
guests of honor at a party that none
of the other guests wanted us invited to.
Only Bighari welcomed us, explaining all
the dinner rituals of Heaven, urging us to try
her favorites among the food for the gods.

At the end of the evening, Bighari linked arms
with Tala, our baby, and now Heaven's baby,
our little star twinkling in the sky.
"Bathala said you start training immediately,"
Bighari said. "I will take you there tomorrow,
bright and early." A knowing nod.

Bighari bade us good night, hugging us each in turn.

"Salamat, Ate!" we all chimed.

"You're always welcome, kapatid.
Good luck out there."

Whose Flame Is the Imprisoned Lightning?

We had entered the Kingdom of Heaven
but found ourselves lost.

Who lifts a lamp for us
beside this golden door?

I.

Our days took shape around learning how
to be immortals, testing out powers

we had been given but never knew we had,
training to fight as if we were never going to die.

We were taught how to be warriors in our father's army
by our brother Kidlat and our sister Anitun.

Kidlat was the eldest son of Bathala;
he crafted lightning bolts as weapons of war.

Kidlat taught us how to run and strike fast,
hitting our opponents when they least expected it.

Anitun Tabu was twin sister to Kidlat;
she used his lightning in her deadliest storms.

Anitun taught us how to raise and gather
the storms within us and deploy them when needed.

I remember the day I showed them
I was learning, perhaps too well.

It had been a long day.
My breaths were shallow, heavy.

"Isa pa," Kidlat demanded. "One more."
He was delighted to witness my fatigue.

I adjusted my shield, braced for impact.
I did not want to be hit again.

Kidlat reached back and drew
a bolt of lightning from the air.

He planted both his feet on the ground and
threw the bolt at me, aiming for my heart.

Kidlat was so sure it would hit and hurt.
I wanted to wipe the smirk off his face.

This time, instead of blocking the bolt,
I caught it with my free hand.

While Kidlat stood astonished,
I hurled the bolt of lightning back,

hitting him square in the chest,
the exact spot where he meant to hit me.

Kidlat staggered, more in shock than pain,
and fell to the ground, clutching his chest.

All of Bathala's children training nearby
stopped what they were doing to stare at me.

Apolaki, eyes wide, looked over at me
from where he was sparring with Anitun.
I nodded.

Stunned silence gave way to whispers: *"Galing!"*
"Was that Mayari?" "Kidlat must be furious."

And then they cheered so loud my ears rang.
And then they clapped me on the back.

II.

Still, we were full of uncertainty; did we belong here?
Could the points between acceptance and belonging
really be so far away from each other?

It was not the cheering crowd who helped me
limp off the field, exhausted, bloody.
It was not the clapping siblings who washed my wounds.
It was Tala who put me back together, as she always did.

That night, like every night, we sat
at the end of Bathala's table.
Only Bighari sat with us, when she was not visiting
Earth to weave more flowers into bahaghari bridges.

Only Bighari always made sure we had enough
to eat at dinner.

Only Bighari truly understood what it felt like
to be alone
even in a room full of people who look like you,
because someone else decides whether or not
you belong,
after your own banish you from the place
you'd called home.

We three clung to Bighari, but Tala was closest to her,
both of them builders of bridges between worlds.
Tala, our baby, was so sweet, so friendly, so bright,
that she was beloved by all who met her.

Even Kidlat would show off to make
Tala and Bighari laugh.

After I hit Kidlat with his own lightning bolt,
he publicly refused to train or advise me.
Apolaki became Kidlat's protégé in everything
from weapon-wielding to boasting.

Anitun set up tests of strength to make me look weak.
Carrying full rain clouds, wrestling hurricanes,
making thunder.

"You're pathetic, hating-tao," she scoffed when I failed.
Again.
"Of course you can't do it, you're half-human."
Laughter.

I vowed to prove that my strength was not in my arms.

III.

One morning, Bathala came to watch us training.
"I saw you beat my general," he said to me, proud.

I blushed, but nodded, then looked at Apolaki.
He was leaning in to listen to Kidlat's whispers.

"You are a brave warrior, Mayari," Bathala said.
"I cannot wait to see what you will do in battle."

Our father talked to me of strategy against
Aman Sinaya, goddess of the seas,
Bathala's eternal nemesis, and our aunt.

I was only half listening, consumed by my worry
that Kuya Apolaki was falling under Kidlat's spell.

Kidlat smiled and winked at me, then turned
to put his arm around Apolaki and led him away.

I burned with a new resolve.
I would become Bathala's general.

I would be the ball of fire in the sky.

Hallowed Be Thy Name

Bathala. Our father.
We had never called him by any other name than
Tatay. Our father.

We called his name when we needed help,
when we needed to feel safe, when we felt lost.
So, too, did our people, our mother Dalisay's people,

the people we now watched over from Heaven,
brown-skinned fishers and farmers, who lived
on the islands protected by the sea goddess Aman Sinaya.

That is, until a new god came to the islands on a boat
from a distant land: a porcelain baby doll,
a cherubic alabaster immigrant in resplendent robes,
given to the highest-ranking mother in the tribe
by alabaster ambassadors.

"This is the Santo Niño," said the ambassadors who
were Catholic priests, misioneros reverently
introducing the baby doll to the tribe's queen.
"He represents the Christ Child, Son of God."

What could the queen do but take the Son of God
into her arms, her heart?
Our people could not refuse the sacred duty
of caring for a child like this.
The priests told us Santo Niño would grow up
only to die for our sins.

The priests told our people to call them "Father"
and taught us a prayer to honor God the Father,
who was in Heaven, whose will was to be done,
who sent His only Son to die for what the priests
kept calling our sins.

The white-skinned people from the boats taught us
many new names for things we had never known

we needed until they told us we did:
spoon, fork, plate, shoes, veil, belt, church, Mass,
confession of our sins.

They gave our people new names, too,
so we would forget what our mothers called us.

Soon our people would forget what our mothers called
everything, even the only Creator God we knew,
whose name we had called when we needed to feel safe,
when we felt lost.

The more our people forgot to
whisper Bathala's name in prayer,
the faster our father began to disappear.
"Remember me," he said one long day, after we had
come back from training in the fields of Heaven.

The days of our life with Bathala were long,
but the years would be short.

For Thine Is the Kingdom

Our father, Bathala, is dying.

He orders the kingdom to gather
in the great hall and summons us,
his three half-mortal children,

to give his blessing,
to grant our inheritance,
to bestow his legacy.

Mayari.
My name means
I am the owner.

Surely Bathala will remember
I am his fiercest warrior.
I am his rightful heir.

"Apolaki!"
Bathala calls my brother to his side.

"One of my strongest,
one of my brightest,
my heir,
my son.

"From now on
your name will be
Araw, the Sun."

I am not sure what is louder:
the cheers ringing in the hall
or the rage drumming in my chest.

"Mayari!"
Bathala should have called me first.

"One of my bravest,
one of my brightest,
my warrior,
my daughter.

"From now on
your name will be
Buan, the Moon."

Is that all I am to do?
Reflect my brother's light?

Bathala forgets
which one of us is
the ball of fire.

I open my mouth
to challenge my brother
for our father's kingdom,

then I hear her name.

Tala . . . *TA-laaah*

And the drums in my heart go quiet.

"Tala!"

Bathala is beaming when he calls her to him.

"My sweetest,

my brightest,

my heart,

my song.

"From now on

your name will mean

Star.

"Every star in Heaven

will twinkle to the tune of

Tala."

The cheers are still ringing in the hall
when I slip out into the night,
fire and blood pounding in my ears.

In the dim moonlight
I see my brother is already
at the great acacia tree.

I go to him and declare the exact time
I will take the throne: "Liwayway."
He scoffs but agrees to meet me at dawn.

I will win tomorrow.

Mama, their names!

Their new names are the same as your middle names!

That's right, Luna.
Your tito, tita, and I were named after
the three half-mortal children of Bathala.
Our lola wanted us to always remember
we are the children of Heaven.

Why did she want that?

Maybe she was worried we would forget
where we came from
once we got to where we were going.
Maybe she liked the way Araw, Buan, and Tala
sounded in her ears,
like wind chimes in the distance.
Maybe she knew we would need our names
to wear as armor when we went through Hell.

Our time in Hell began on a hot Sunday in August, right after Church . . .

We Interrupt This Program

We are in Lola Lusing's living room after Church,
Kuya Jojo, Kuya Nes, Ate Didi, Tala, and me,
sprawled on the floor with our uncle,
watching TV and playing pick-up sticks.

Tito Boy is really good at pick-up sticks,
but he always lets Tala win because she is the baby.

He is our favorite uncle,
the youngest of Lola Lusing's kids,
a handsome bachelor who dates mestizas,
works in an office in Makati City, drives a Japanese car.

Tito Boy helps us practice our English,
even teaching us curse words that make our titas frown.

Today, on this hot, sticky August Sunday,
our uncle is explaining to us what "assassinate" means.

"They just left him on the tarmac," Tito Boy says.
"Ninoy was finally coming home, to lead us again.
Marcos and his cronies are animals!
They won't ever admit it, but we all know it was th—"

"Tama na, Boy," Lola Lusing interrupts firmly.
"That's enough. Turn off the TV and take the kids out."

She holds out a fifty-peso bill to him. "Para sa ice cream."
Lola waves the bill, using her pursed lips
to point to the door.

"Pero Ma—" Tito Boy tries to object, but
Lola stops sorting rice in her shallow basket,
stands up from the sofa, and turns off the TV herself.
Her lips point firmly to the door again: "Go."

At the school playground, we all sit in a row
on the sidewalk, eating our cones,
Tala and me sharing our different-flavored ice creams,
while Tito Boy runs his fingers through his hair, paces.

Ninoy must have been important
to our uncle and his activist friends;
the news of his death had interrupted
a new episode of *Mazinger-Z*.

Fight or Flight

It begins as a fad: everyone wearing yellow pins
that blare *Laban!*—Fight!
None of us knew how we would fight, we just knew
we would when called.

We salute each other as fellow revolutionaries
in the streets of Manila
by making the L sign with our index finger and thumb.
Laban!

Ever the entrepreneur, Kuya Nes buys *Laban!*
pins in bulk and sells them at a profit
on the playgrounds and at the protest marches.

Then the marches get so big, they close down
Ayala Avenue in Makati City.

Mom lets me make giant banners of support
from recycled dot matrix printer paper.
I unfurl my creations out the twelfth-story window of
her office building and shout *"Laban!"*
to marchers, waving happily like I would at any parade.

We tie yellow ribbons around trees and lampposts
to honor Ninoy, the conquering hero
who came home and died for someone else's sins.

Then my parents start talking about something they call
a visa lottery, where the prize is not money, but
freedom: a one-way ticket to America.

"Too bad they already called our number."
Mom and Dad had said no in 1978 when offered
a chance to leave the Philippines
with a newborn and two young kids.

Our life under Marcos then was not yet something to
run from. We were safe, even though martial law
had meant curfews, water and electricity rations, protests.

Now, five years later, everything's changed.
Rolling blackouts are more frequent,
protests are becoming violent,
more resisters and journalists have begun disappearing.

Our nannies start turning off the radio
whenever the news comes on. "Too scary."
Soon, there is chismis about girls
disappearing from our barrio.

Ate Inday doesn't know that I heard her whispering
with the Jacintos' yaya. "Watch Elsie and Tala closely.
They are so pretty and mestiza. The bosses like that."

Then my parents get news that our number was called
for the visa lottery. "Again?"
A clerical error in our favor. "Thank God!"
As if God has power over bureaucracy.

Mom and Dad accept what might have been someone
else's golden ticket, someone else's chance at freedom.
"Clearly, God intends for us to go to America."

None of us thought we could choose not to fight, but
now we have been called.
Our family takes off our yellow *Laban!*
pins and prepares to flee, to fly.

How old were you then, Mama?

I was your age, Stella. Just nine years old.
Tito Nes was twelve, Tita Tala was six.

You know, the first time I ever wrote
my name in cursive was to sign
my Immigrant Passport for America.

Wow, really? We're learning cursive now. It's hard.

It can be, and you'll probably use it less than I do now.
I mostly use cursive when I sign my name.

Anyway, it was a few months before we left for
America . . .

Sign Your Name

My full given name is
Maria Elsaleta Buan Garcia Aguila,
but everyone calls me Elsie.

My mother gave me my name
when she gave birth to me, and
now she is asking me to sign it.

"Not just print it,"
she says, sighing loudly.
"Sign it, anak. In cursive."

I don't know what "cursive" means.
I don't know how to do what Mom wants.
I don't know what I'm signing.

"Immigration Passport mo ito,"
she says, then adds more softly,
"We leave for America real soon."

Mom makes me practice writing my name
over and over on a piece of paper
until it looks just right.

"You can only sign it one time,"
she warns, as kindly as she can.
"Kailangan perfect."

I know how to write my name now.
I know I have to sign it to make it official.
I know who I am and where I have to go.

Fifty Pounds

Mom says
we are to bring only
our most precious belongings.

Today we are packing for America.

Mom says
we are allowed
just fifty pounds each.

"Take only what you can carry."

Fifty pounds
in metric units
is twenty-three kilos.

That's how much I weighed at my last checkup.

One box
One suitcase
One me

"Will I be your fifty pounds, Mom?"

Mom *hmphs* and her hand reaches for me.
I flinch, but she just smooths my furrowed brow.
"Cute mo naman," she says.

"You are not counted as baggage, anak."

I feel a little better
but a not-so-small part of me
doesn't believe her.

She has never asked me if I *want* to go to America.

But Mama, don't you like America?

Of course I do, baby. I love America. I love being here.
If I hadn't come to America,
I would never have met Daddy.
I would not have had you and Ate Luna.

But I was just your age, and I had to leave my home.
I had to leave everything and everyone I loved.

If I asked you right now to move to another country,
what would you say? Would you jump up and say yes?

Move there? We can't just visit there first?

I didn't visit America before we moved here.

Could I take all my video games?

No. You can take only what you can carry.

Hmmm . . .

What did you take, Mama?

Take Only What You Can Carry

I want to take my bedroom,
my bed with Little Twin Stars pillows,
my favorite books and *Darna Komix,*
my dolls from around the world.

Daddy always brings me dolls
as pasalubong after his business trips.
I want to take my favorite dolls,
the one with yellow hair, blue eyes, wooden shoes;
the one with red hair, green eyes, bagpipes;
the one with black hair, brown eyes like mine, a guitar.

"Ang ganda nilang lahat, 'no?" Daddy once said.
Yes, they are all so beautiful.

I want to take our playground set,
the seesaw where we pretend we're flying,
the metal slide that burns our bums if the sun is out,

the swing that hit Tala in the mouth
and chipped her tooth.

Daddy must have known the langka tree
he planted would grow over the slide for shade.

I want to take all of Rosal Street,
from Kaunlaran public school,
where I went to kindergarten,
to Lola's compound, with her bougainvillea bushes,

to the corner sari-sari store that sells
Sarsi Cola in a baggie with a straw.

Daddy always buys me Sarsi to sip during our walks.
"Finish it before we get home, okay?"

I want to take Ayala Alabang Village,
the community center, where
we have potluck lunches after Church,
my best friend Valerie's house, where
we make our Barbies kiss,
the Visayas Street creek, where we catch frogs.

Kuya Nes usually catches the most frogs,
but Daddy says I get the best jumpers.

I want to take our cousins' house,
their courtyard, where we once
ate all the guavas and got sick,
Ate Didi's bedroom, where we go
to hide from our older brothers,

their veranda, where we sit on the swing
while our dads drink their San Miguel.

I will take all of this and carry it in my heart.
It is heavier than fifty pounds.

Yayas

Our nannies have washed,
folded, and packed
most of our clothes.

Our family leaves
for America tomorrow.

Our yayas will not be going
and we are in their room, sad.

Ate Celine is ironing
our shirts and pants
like we are going to Church
instead of a new country.

Her eyes are puffy
like the time she told me
her high school boyfriend
had married someone else.

I sit on Ate Celine's bunk
reading the latest *Kislap* tabloid,
Snooky and Gabby on the cover,
my favorite star couple.

Ate Inday and Tala
snuggle on the bottom bunk,
crying together.

"May *Yagit* ba sa Amerika?"

Ate Inday wonders if
their favorite soap opera
is on TV in our new country.

"Magpakabait ka, ha?"
Ate Inday says between sobs.
Tala nods, promises
she will be a good girl.

Ate Celine gives me a yellow wallet,
Snooky's photo on the front,
a single peso inside.

I give her a big hug and wonder
if our mother will read *Kislap* with us
if our mother will watch *Yagit* with us
if our mother will learn how to raise us.

I wonder if our mother will know us,
if our mother will love us like our yayas
when we are in a new home
just us, alone, without our yayas.

The Happiest Place on Earth

On the fifth day in our new country,
Tita Belen takes us to Disneyland.

It is everything we had ever dreamed America would be:
clean, bright, and full of blond and blue-eyed people,
sweet treats, cartoon characters, fun rides, new friends.

We take a photo with Mickey Mouse,
who we know is a guy in a costume,
and whose white-gloved hands could
easily cover my entire head.
Mickey's plastic smile is more real—is this real?—
than *our* nervous smiles.

Tita Belen was our auntie by neighborhood, not by blood.
She moved to Los Angeles ten years before us.
Tita Belen has a big house, a pool, American citizenship,
cable TV, a Mercedez Benz.

And on the seventh day, her daughter teaches me about
Duran Duran.

"Want to watch MTV?" Leni asks us.
Kuya, Tala, and I look to one another.
"Oh, you guys don't know what MTV is. Here."
Leni turns on the TV.

The "Reflex" video is an electronic light show
put on by pretty boys, all highlighted hair,
eyeliner, tight pants, and shoulder pads.

I don't know what to make of it until they sing
"They're watching . . ."
and the bass player looks directly at the camera,
through the screen, into my soul.

"That's John Taylor," Leni says when she catches me
staring at the screen.

I nod but keep staring, waiting for another long glimpse
at John Taylor.
He is cuter than the cutest stars back home,
even Gabby Concepcion.

I don't know what to say, but I think that
America might be all right
if all the boys here are
even half as good-looking as
this John Taylor.

Who's Gabby Concepcion?

He was a teen movie star back in the Philippines.
He was *really* cute and I had a *huge* crush on him.

EEW!

You say that now, but someday you might
get crushes on boys, too.

NEVER.

Ha! I'll remember you said that when
you get your first crush, Luna.

Mama, could I go get a glass of water?

I know you, Stella Miller.
You will take forever in the kitchen.
I'll go get it and be right back.
I want a cup of tea anyway.

Thanks, Mama . . .
Hey, Ate Luna, heads up!

Ow, Stella! You hit me right in the face with that pillow!
Give it to me.

No! Give it back! I said give it back! Maaamaaa!

Hey! Stop it before one of you puts an eye out!
I leave for one minute and you're trying to kill each other.

Ate Luna took my pillow!

Well, you hit me with it!
Hey! I was sitting next to Mama! Move!

NO, YOU MOVE!

NO, YOU!

Tama na! That's enough from both of you! Hoy!
HOY!
I said, "Stop it before one of you puts an eye out!"

Why do you always say that, Mama?
You and Tita and Tito fought all the time.
Nobody ever put their eyes out. Like, ever in history.
It doesn't happen.

Oh, but it did happen.
Once upon a time.
In the blink of an eye.

Mayari learned this the hard way,
when she met her brother for battle.

Liwayway

At night when I sat
sentinel inside myself,
I would touch my only eye
and remember the darkest day.

In my mind's eye, I'd see three children.
They were fighting, loving, forgiving.
Their bonds were forged with blood.

It is just before dawn.
I am waiting for my brother
at the great acacia tree.

I grip my staff and check the bolo at my hip.

I.

I see him sauntering down the hill.
I narrow my eyes and grit my teeth,
impatient at his casual approach.

"You ready to lose so early?" he says.

Araw twirls his cudgel,
props it on his shoulder,
yawns and stretches.

I want to wipe the smirk off his face.

Fighting is like dancing to death
and we dance and we dance
for what feels like hours, days.

I want what is rightfully mine, what I own.

I swing my staff twice:
hit Araw's left cheek, then his right.
Before he can raise his cudgel again, I sweep his leg
and he falls on his back, his eyes growing wide with fear.

Bathala made me his general after seeing me
dance like this in battle.

Suddenly it feels like time has slowed down.
I see my undoing happen before my eyes
as if it were happening to someone else.

I am outside my body somehow, watching myself.

Araw scrambles to his feet, fumbles for his cudgel
but, like Kidlat with his lightning bolt, I am precise.
I use my staff to poke through his hand and flip his
cudgel away.

From somewhere in the distance I hear Tala's voice.

"Ate! Kuya! NO!
Tama na! Enough!"
I turn to see her shooting down the hill.

I will myself back into my body, but it is too late.

Araw is already running toward me,
sweaty, bloody body glistening,
mouth twisted, eyes ablaze.

I do not get my staff up in time.

Isang kisapmata.
One blink of an eye.
That's all he needed.

II.

All I can see is black.
Hasn't the sun risen?
I fall to the ground.

I feel Tala take my head in her lap.
I hear her crying, asking, "Bakit, Kuya?"
I want to know why she's asking him why.

Do I hear Araw crying, too?
Am I crying?
Are my eyes closed?

In my mind's eye, I see three children laughing.
They are radiant, content, sitting in a circle.
They are us, in the fields with Nanay and Tatay.

"I am so sorry," my brother sobs.
"How could you?" my sister seethes.
"What's happening?" I whisper.

My brother and sister do not answer.
I put a hand up to my face.
I know it is not wet with tears.

I pull my hand away.
I'm holding an eye.
I'm holding my own eye.

All I can see is red.
Where is my staff?
I never even unsheathed my bolo.

Isang kisapmata.
One blink of an eye.
One bloody eye.

III.

Our father is dying.
Our mother is dead.
Our world is changing.

I challenged my brother
for the Kingdom of Heaven
and I lost.

"Tama na," Araw murmurs,
wiping tears and blood
from his face and mine.

"Enough," he says again, a little louder.
"Let us share our father's kingdom.
Let us take turns sitting on our throne."

"So, no *Agawang Sulok?*" I wink with my only eye.
I make light of this, the darkest situation;
always feels better to laugh than to cry.

In my mind's eye, I see three grown children laughing.
We are exhausted, bloody, sitting in a circle.
Tala is holding both Araw's hand and mine.

"I rule during the day," Araw declares.
"Under my eyes, our people grow food, stay warm.
I am father of the earth."

"I rule during the night," I say. Tala shines at my side.

"Under my eye, our people fall asleep in gentle light.

I am mother of the ocean."

Isang kisapmata

One blink of an eye.
All it takes to drift into dreams.
Sweet dreams, my hearts.

One more story, Mama?

It's very late, anak. Go to sleep.

Can we sleep in your bed, Mama?

Not tonight, baby.

Awww. Why not?

It's hard for me and Daddy to sleep
when you're in our bed.

Somehow you always manage
to spread out like a starfish
and we get just a sliver of bed by morning.

That's not me; that's her!

It's both of you!

No! Hey! No tickling, Mama.
You're the one who said
we had to stop playing games.

And you also said you would tell us
more of your family's story. Isa pa!

You're right. Okay, isa pa. One more.
A story that reflects Mayari's tale.

This is my Aguila family's story
about looking for Heaven on Earth.
And it begins in a basement in Jersey City.

Jack-en-Poy

Time for bed means time to win
Jack-en-poy!
I throw my scissors.
Kuya Nes throws rock.
Isa pa!

Mom and Dad spread out
comforters and blankets,
hand-me-downs
from our landlord.

Tala has a special assignment;
she is in charge of arranging the pillows
so our heads are toward the sofa
and our feet are toward the sink.

Once more.
Jack-en-poy!
I throw paper.
Kuya throws rock.
Isa pa! Tiebreaker na 'to!

Mom and Dad spread out
the second layer of blankets,
wrap them around the post in the middle
of our one-room basement home.

Tiebreaker.
Jack-en-poy!
I throw paper.
Kuya throws scissors.
KUUUYAAA!!!

In the dim moonlight
shining through our
two half-windows
I see him stretch out his legs
like a smug starfish.

I stick my tongue out at him.
PBBBLT!!!
I turn slowly away, careful
not to bash my toes against the post.
Again.

I will win tomorrow.

I'll Be Home for Christmas

One of my earliest memories, in our Alabang house:
decorating our Christmas tree with Kuya and Tala
while *The Carpenters Christmas* album plays.

Mom knows every word and sings happily, sweetly,
sounding just like Karen Carpenter, like an angel.
"I'll be home for Christmas. You can plan on me."

1. Please have snow

It is bedtime and we are in our pajamas.
Kuya Nes and I are brushing our teeth
while Tala reads with Dad in the living room.

Mom reminds us to lay out our uniforms:
"Where are your leg warmers, Elsie? Ah, there.
It's freezing out and supposed to snow tomorrow."

I'm looking in the drawers for my and Tala's gloves
when I hear Tala call out: "Ate! Kuya! SNOW!"
We rush out to the living room. SNOW!

Tala is jumping up and down. "Can you believe it?!"
Dad is standing by the window, a wide grin on his face.
Even Mom looks excited to see snow falling.

Tala asks Mom, "Please can we go outside?"
Mom purses her lips, but Tala's eyes are too bright.
"Ay sige na nga," Mom relents. "But put on your coats!"

At ten o'clock at night on December 4, 1984,
the Aguilas of Jersey City have a snowball fight
dressed in pajamas, knit hats, winter coats, and boots.

It is the first time any of us has ever seen or felt snow.
It is the last time any of us get Mom to play.

11. Christmas Eve will find me

It's Christmas Eve, and we go to the early Mass;
Mom doesn't want to walk to Church at night
through our snow-covered neighborhood.

I remember our last Christmas back home,
our last Simbang Gabi at St. Anthony's Parish,
just a few months before we left for America.

I remember being hurried up the church steps
after I stopped to smell the yumminess wafting
from the street vendors' carts just outside.

I remember fidgeting more than usual during Mass,
knowing that just beyond the heavy gilded doors
were my favorites: bibingka, puto bumbong, pastillas.

I can almost taste that heavenly first bite
of piping-hot bibingka, the best reward
for living through a nearly two-hour Mass.

Outside Our Lady of Victories Church,
there are no vendors selling bibingka,
puto bumbong, pastillas, or any other treats.

There is only a lot of snow, making sidewalks slippery.
There is only a lot of dirty, mushy snow.

III. If only in my dreams

Our landlord lives downstairs on the first floor.
Not only is he Pinoy, he's also from Dad's province.
He was kind enough to invite us to Noche Buena tonight.

Except for Mass, Mom's whole day was devoted
to making pancit, which she only makes for parties.
Downstairs, she places it beside the lumpia
at the food table.

After Kuya, Tala, and I go with Mom and Dad to greet
our hosts, we three check out the dessert table and
I'm excited to find not only bibingka and puto bumbong,
but also three kinds of pastillas.

We eat until we are full to bursting
(I sample all the pastillas).
Mom joins karaoke for one rendition of "Dahil Sa Iyo"
before she gives Dad the signal that she is ready to go
home.

I know it will take at least half an hour
for the two of them to say goodbye to our hosts,
their whole family, and everyone they met,
so I help our landlady make our family to-go plates.

We go back upstairs and Mom puts on
The Carpenters Christmas.
She sits down with Dad on the couch
and he puts his arm around her.
"I'll Be Home for Christmas" comes on.
"Mom's favorite," I think.

Suddenly, Mom gets up from the couch
and goes toward the bathroom.
Dad tries to follow her, but she waves him off.
He looks at me, shrugs.

I creep up a minute later.
Mom has left the bathroom door ajar. I peek in.

I see my mother crying into a dark blue towel
dotted with tiny yellow stars.
It is the first time I realize we may never again
be home for Christmas.

Mama, is that why Christmas Eve is so special to you?

It's definitely one of the reasons, yeah.
In the Philippines, we even opened our gifts
on Christmas Eve, after Noche Buena.

Wait, but what about the gifts that Santa brings?

Oh Stella! Pilipinos don't have chimneys, so they d—

Luna.

What? Oh.

Ate, what?

Um, by the way, Mama, before I forget,
could you please drive me to school tomorrow?

Luna Miller, it is two blocks to the bus stop.
You can walk.

But I have my presentation tomorrow!
That means I have to lug my big board!

Ate Luna, what were you going to say about chimneys?
How does Santa get presents to kids in the Philippines?

OH-EM-GEE. Magic, okay, Stella? MAGIC.
Mama, please drive me just to the bus stop, then?

Fine. Just to the bus stop. Hmph.
When I was your age, I walked *all the way* to school.
Almost a mile in Jersey City! Even in the snow!

Was it uphill both ways?

Girl, you're about to lose your ride.

Hee! Sorry! I was just joking.

Now you have to pay a tickle tax.

Maamaa!

Thy Will Be Done

Tonight is the first night of summer vacation.

Mom says we have to
pray the rosary together
every night after dinner.

Kuya and I tilt our heads
just enough to see each other's eyes
roll ever so slightly upward.

When we mumble our protest
Mom purses her lips,
stabs at the chicken on her plate.

"Don't you want God to give us a house?"

I do want a house of our own
with a big backyard
where I can cartwheel on the grass.

After dinner, we kneel at the altar,
Tala between Mom and Dad,
Kuya and me behind them.

He is already making faces at me.
I'm coughing from stifling laughter.
Tala keeps sneaking looks back at us.

The first Sorrowful Mystery
is the Agony in the Garden.

One Our Father
Ten Hail Marys
One Glory Be

The second Sorrowful Mystery
is the Scourging at the Pillar.

Kuya pinches me, lightning fast. "Oww!"
Mom whips her head around.
Kuya smirks, eyes up front.

The third Sorrowful Mystery
is the Crowning with Thorns.

Now I have to pee.
I can tell Tala does, too.
We are both sighing extra loud.

The fourth Sorrowful Mystery
is the Carrying of the Cross.

"Mom, I have to pee."
"We only have one more Mystery to go!"
It's hard to cross your legs when you're kneeling.

The fifth Sorrowful Mystery
is the Crucifixion and Death of our Lord.

Through the window I see Denise outside
practicing Mary Lou Retton's gymnastics floor routine.
She's getting better than me at balancing.

Hail, Holy Queen, Mother of mercy.
Hail, our life, our sweetness, and our hope.
To thee do we cry, poor banished children of Eve.
To thee do we send up our sighs,
mourning and weeping in this valley of tears.

I can't stop myself from praying in my head,
"God and Mama Mary, please give us a house already.
I can't do this EVERY. SINGLE. NIGHT."

Pray for us, O holy Mother of God.
That we may be made worthy of the promises of Christ.

When we cross ourselves a final time,
I nearly shout "AMEN!" and scramble to my feet.
I outrun Tala to the bathroom (ha!) and go quickly.

Then I run down the street, but Denise is already gone.
Mary Lou Retton must have to practice alone all the time.
I practice balancing on the bricks until it is dark outside.

Walter

Walter is the only white person
with a house on our block.
He lives around the corner
on the way to ShopRite.

Walter is retired;
his wife died about ten years back.
His kids are all grown, have families,
moved to much better neighborhoods.

Walter knows everyone on our block.
Never lets you pass his house without a "Howdy!"
He always sits on his stoop, rain or shine,
and waves at all the neighbors.

Our neighbors are nice enough, but
they are not our cousins or uncles or aunties.
Mom and Dad work too much to make friends.
We would not meet another Tita Belen here.

Kuya has gotten into a few fights at school
with boys who call us new, ugly, hurtful names.
I met a new girl named Valerie; I hoped we'd be friends
but she thinks Little Twin Stars is for babies.

Tala has to take English as a Second Language classes
even though we have been speaking English for years
because people who look like Walter had taught us
that the only dream worth dreaming is American.

Today, we decide we've had enough of
this American life.
So we pack our bags
after Mom and Dad leave for work.

Kuya packs our clothes and jackets.
I pack SPAM-and-egg sandwiches, snacks.
Tala packs our favorite toys.
We are going to take the bus into Manhattan.

After lunch we write
a goodbye note to Mom and Dad,
then walk toward the bus station,
a little ways past ShopRite.

Walter waves to us from his front stoop. "Howdy!"
We wave back and try to keep walking faster,
but he calls our names. An elder calls you, you answer.

"Where you kids headed?" he asks. Casual.
Tala and I look at Kuya, our leader.
"We're running away," Kuya answers. Defiant.

Walter's face does not change.
"I see. You gonna catch a bus or somethin'?"
All three of us look at one another and nod.

"You kids got enough food?" Walter asks.
Blue is the color of kindness in his eyes.

"We have sandwiches, chips, and fruit."
Tala mouths "yum" when Kuya says "fruit."

"Good. But it's a long walk to the station.
Maybe you should have a snack first."

We look nervously at one another.
Eight blocks *is* a long walk.

"I just made cookies. Right out of the oven."
Cookies! Warm, homemade cookies!

"What do you think? Cookies first?" Nods.
 "All right then. Come on in."

Over cookies, we talk about life on the road.
Then we help Walter wash and dry our milk glasses.

Out the window, the sun is getting low in the sky.
Mom and Dad will be home at six.

"It'll be dark soon," Walter says,
a nod toward the window.
"You'd best get going. Catch your bus."

"Well . . . um . . . it might be hard for us," Kuya says,
"to find our way in the dark." A slow exhale.

"You're right," Walter says. "Better to head out
tomorrow, bright and early." A knowing nod.

Walter walks us out and unlatches his gate.
"Thanks, Walter!" we all chime.

"You're always welcome, kids.
Good luck out there."

Back Home

As soon as we get back from Walter's house
Kuya Nes grabs our goodbye note off the hall table.
"Throw it away," he quietly instructs me.

I nod but put the note in my pocket.
I tell Tala to put away what we had packed.
I start the rice for dinner, like I do every day.

Mom and Dad get home from work, right on time.
Mom makes pork adobo with monggo guisado. We eat
as if we had not just tried to run away from all this.

I.

I am lying in my bottom bunk, all covers off.
It's hot and humid in Jersey City, almost like home.
Tala climbs down from her bed and snuggles me.

"Aiii, Tala. It's too hot," I complain.

"Ate, will we try to run away again tomorrow?"

"I don't think so," I say, unsure. I yawn. She yawns.

Tala has finally fallen asleep, so I slip out
of my bed and carefully lift the edge of the mattress
where I hid the note we had left for Mom and Dad.

II.

Dear Mom and Dad,
(Kuya wrote in cursive),
We are sorry we had to leave.

We tried our best to live here,
to be American on the outside,
but Pinoy pa rin on the inside.

The kids at school will always
find new things wrong with us,
find new reasons not to be our friends.

Kids call me "chink" and "monkey."
I fight to defend myself like Dad says
I should, but I'm smaller than other boys.

Elsie and Tala are having trouble
making friends because you won't let them
do slumber parties. Girls love slumber parties!

We know it's hard at home right now,
but at least there nobody will tell us
to go back to where we came from.

We have enough food and clothes
for a few days, and we will work,
maybe somewhere in the city,

maybe just until we have enough
to buy plane tickets back to Manila,
then we'll call Tito Boy to pick us up.

You raised us to take care of ourselves
and each other, so it's time for us
to prove we can do that on our own.

We love you, Mom and Dad.
Maybe we will see you back home.

—Nes

III.

I tear the note up after reading it,
and wipe away my tears. I breathe out,
and climb back into bed with Tala.

"Ate Elsie, did you know
that frogs say *ribbit* here
and not *kokak* like at home?"

"That's not true.
I hear frogs say *kokak*
here all the time."

"Maybe your ears
are too Pilipino still."

"Maybe your ears
are becoming American."

IV.

Like in so many faerie tales,
we are magic frogs who speak,
secret warrior princesses.

We are bilingual frogs who sing
our wishes for a happy ending,
and still all I hear is *kokak*.

Heaven Is a Place on Earth

Every year Mom reminds us that we are not from here.
At once sounding wistful, regretful, and frustrated,
she says, "On this day we arrived in America." A sigh.

She writes the number of years on the calendar
in Sharpie, like a prisoner would mark
every day on the wall of their cell.
"Can you believe it's been four years na?" Another sigh.

I.

Every day, Mom and Dad long for the Philippines,
yet whenever Kuya Nes, Tala, and I misbehave,
they clench their fists and teeth, threatening us:
"Do you want to go back home? We can send you back."

I look at Kuya Nes whenever they do this,
and I know he knows I want to say "Then send us back!"

and I know he knows I read his goodbye note,
because he nods at me, then rolls his eyes.

Offenses that could get us sent back include
making too much noise in the apartment at night,
fighting over who gets to pick a cartoon next,
not eating food our cousins could only wish to waste.

Mom and Dad remind us what was back home,
what we left behind to come to America:
"Riots, blackouts, water rations. Girls disappearing."

All we have to face here in our new home
is not having friends, not fitting in at school,
getting beat up: "First World problems."
Kuya and I close our eyes.

II.

At lunchtime, we open up our leftovers wrapped in foil
and kids say in not-so-secret whispers: *"Gross!"*
"Why do you eat rice at lunch?" "I'd never eat SPAM."

"Please, Mom.

Pack us peanut butter and jelly sandwiches."

"No. That is junk food."

"But that's what American kids eat."

"Well, you are not American. Pilipinos eat Pilipino food."

Still, Mom slowly starts making more American food,
but she overcooks steak and undercooks potatoes.
At least she finally makes us PBJs for lunch once a week.

III.

During our first two years in America, we move
from the basement to a two-bedroom upstairs,
where the three of us share a room, then to a new city,
where the three of us still have to share a room.

It's our third year in America, where we are not from,
and God finally answers our countless rosary prayers.

We are moving into a row home
with a tiny yard in Baltimore.
Of course Kuya Nes, the oldest, the son,
gets his own room.

Mom believes God gave us the house we prayed for,
but we all know this house Dad's three jobs paid for.
Now he can cut back to two jobs, stop working on
Sundays.

I hope soon Dad can just have one job.
It will feel like winning the lottery.
Again.

IV.

After five years of living, working, paying taxes
in America, we have been given the chance
to become American citizens.

In a courtroom in downtown Baltimore,
we stand with fellow immigrants
from around the world, raise our right hands

and say the Pledge of Allegiance to the flag
of the United States.
Then the judge tells us we must renounce
all our other allegiances.

"Now you are not Filipino, Chinese, Japanese,
Vietnamese, or Indian.
Not Italian, Irish, Scottish, or German. Now you are
all just American."
I look over at my parents, expecting them to be happy,
celebrating the acceptance granted by
an official document declaring them American.

Mom starts crying silently, as do other mothers,
right hands raised.
Hadn't we already given up all we had to be here,
to become American?

Why couldn't we be Vietnamese, Chinese, Japanese, Pilipino,
Indian, Italian, Irish, Scottish, or German and also
American?

V.

Did we really want to belong to a country that
did not know or want us as we are,
did not consider the weight of our hearts

did not want to see the color of our skin,
did not find beauty in the shape of our eyes,
did not understand the sound of our songs?

How could the points
between acceptance and belonging
be so far away from each other?

A Problem Like Maria

Today is the first day of school.

We have to walk about a mile to
Cardinal Shehan Elementary
from the row home we were able to buy in Baltimore.
Mom doesn't drive and Dad uses our only car for work.
We walk past Giant grocery store,
past Good Samaritan Hospital,
and down a steep hill that can get slippery in winter.

Every year, going to school reminds me that
we are not from here.
Every teacher calls me Maria.
It's not my true name, nor my birth name.

I feel like I lost my names
during the journey between countries.
I feel like I lost my voice
in the ocean between continents.

When I started fifth grade last year,
I asked for my name back,
because nobody calls me Maria except
Mom when she's mad,
because I've been Elsie since birth, even to
my teachers back home.

Mrs. Schraeder said, "We've been calling you Maria
for almost a year. We don't want everyone to have to
remember a new name. Do we?"
She looked at me in a way that silences all answers
except "No, ma'am."

Maybe if I make my voice stronger, louder,
they will all be forced to listen, to pay attention when
I take my name back.

Sister Teresa tells us the story of Jesus changing Simon's
name to Peter, then she asks if we have questions.
I immediately raise my hand to ask,

"Did Jesus ask Simon
if he was okay with being called Peter?"

"Oh, Maria." A sigh. "Go see Sister Patricia." *Oooh.*
"Now."

I get up from my seat and walk past Lindsay,
who rolls her eyes at me.

"Why, Maria?" Sister Patricia asks when I am in the
principal's office. "This is the second time
this month you are here for your . . . questions."

"I don't understand. Why can't I ask it?
It's a real question."

"Not in religion class!" Sister says, a little too loudly.

"Then when may I ask, Sister? When?"
I ask, just as loudly.

Sister Patricia does not answer.
She inhales and exhales, long and slow breaths.
She starts arranging papers on her desk,
straightening pencils in the cup.

I feel my heart beating all the way through my fingers,
which start to curl in on themselves,
making my hands into the shape of my heart.

"Why doesn't anyone believe me when I say that
my name is Elsie?"

I've asked this question before, but
never have my words been so clear,
never has my voice been this steady,
never have I burned with such resolve.

"Oh, Maria." A sigh. Sister Patricia takes off her glasses
and rubs her eyes.

"Sister, I said my name is El—" She holds up a hand,
then points to the door.

I wait until I'm almost to the stairs before I allow
my smile to shine.

Everyone calls you Elsie now

Yes, they do. I learned how to tell people
who I really am from the start.

I didn't know living in America was so hard for you.

Sometimes it still is . . . but it's a little bit easier, now.
I've learned that it's more than okay to speak up,
to tell people my true name, speak with my true voice.
Moving here was the right thing for us to do.

But you had to leave everything you knew behind.

I didn't leave *everything* I knew.
I still know exactly who I am.
Maybe I have always known.

You're Elsaleta Buan Aguila Miller.

You're our mama.

Always.

Do you think Buan ever forgave Dalisay?

I know she did, as we all forgive those we love most.
But she never forgot.

Nanay

At night when I sat
sentinel inside myself
I drew your memory around me.

Nanay, when I thought of your last touch,
the slap weighs heavy on my shoulders,
a quilt drawn too close and hot
but too familiar to shrug off,

then your name is a stone
in my mouth, such a curse
I dare not say aloud.

But when I think of how you really said goodbye,
brushed hair away from my eyes,
tucked it behind my ear . . . a reminder
to be watchful, to listen well,

then your name is coconut water
on my tongue, cool and lightly sweet,
a song, a lullaby.

And so it is that sometimes
I still call your name in the middle of the night
when I am alone,
when I am tired,
when I most need you.

For who knows the sweet burden of watching
over your beloveds as they sleep, hoping
that they will wake in the morning and
be safe,
be loved,
be well.

For who knows how to carry that burden
but a mother, a sister who mothers,
my sister, my mother.

And so I sing out in the night

Nanay . . . *NAH-nigh*

By Any Other Name

"Nanay" in Tagalog means
"Mother" in English means
"Mama" in Millerese.

When you were born, moonbeam,
I introduced myself to you:
"Hey, Luna. I am Mama."

When you were born, starshine,
I introduced myself to you:
"Hi, Stella. I am Mama."

I.

They say that when you name it
you claim it, and I named myself
Mama rather than Mommy.

A woman I once called Mommy
who sang the world to life for me,
whose heart was shaped like a fist,
taught me that I could not call that name

when I needed help,
when I needed to feel safe,
when I felt lost.

I claimed a new name for mother
to claim myself as yours, always.
I know my name is safe in your mouths.

II.

They say having a child
is like having your heart
walk around outside your body.

Having you, my children,
is like growing two new hearts,
watching you from inside my body.

I know my heart is a muscle
the size of my fist.

I learned how to open both,
keep loving, keep fighting.

I had to find the mother I needed in sisters
whose faces and voices fill my heart,
who touch my life with open hands.

I found the mother I needed in myself,
when you are frightened and I hold you
close to my heart and coo,

"It's okay. Mama is here."

What about when you can't be here, Mama?

What do Daddy and I always say about our family?

We're Team Miller.

You and Ate Luna will always be part of a team.
Just like Tita Tala and I are always part of a team.
Just like Buan and Tala were always part of a team.

And what do teammates do?

We show up for each other.
We work together.
We help each other be our best.

Amazing! You two were actually listening.
For once.

Maamaa!

Okay, seriously. I want you to remember
and tell me about one time you showed up
for each other, as teammates, as sisters.

I remember when I fell off the couch
when I was five, and I cried a lot.
Stella, you brought me my Pooh Bear.

I remember that, too. Stella, that was very kind.

Well, I wanted Ate Luna to feel better.

I did, after I cried into Pooh Bear a little more.

I remember when we were redoing our room last year.
Mama, you asked me and Ate if we wanted bunk beds.

And you totally said no. It was so cute.

Yeah, I liked sleeping with our beds pushed together.
Then I could snuggle up to you like this.

Aww, Stelly Belly! You're my little baby star.

Home Is Where the Heart Is

Having two children helps me understand
how I can call two places home,
how I can love more than one country
with all my heart.

I.

For years I searched for my mother;
not the mother of my birth, but
the mother of my heart.

I searched for her in every heart-to-heart,
listened carefully to the rhythm, hoping to hear:

You're safe.
Thump thump.
You're safe.

Thump thump.
You're safe.

For years I longed for a motherland
that only existed in my memories and dreams,
that only lives on in songs and stories.

I searched for a place where I would belong,
listening hopefully for a heart to sing back to mine:

You're home.
Thump thump.
You're home.
Thump thump.
You're home.

When I could count my age on my fingers,
I thought that I belonged somewhere as long as
I lived someplace for a while or
I spoke the same language or
I ate, prayed, loved like everyone else.

As I ran out of fingers to count my age,
I learned that even when I think I belong,
someone else can decide I do not,
someone else makes the rules of belonging,
someone else certain of their authority can tell me,

"Go back to where you came from."

How can I go back to where I came from
when even in my mother's arms I am unsafe?

How can I go back to where I came from
when even in my motherland I am unsafe?

II.

Sometimes I think about what life would have been like
if we had decided to go back to the Philippines or
if we had decided not to leave at all.

I would not have been free to write of
dissent and resistance,

to speak for sisters and brothers who
can't speak for themselves.

I would not have been free to make choices
about my own body,
to have you, my hearts, only when I decided I was ready.
I would not have been free to love and marry your father,
and together choose whether or not
we call any gods by name.

And if I had fought for these freedoms, if I had dared
to oppose a dictator and government that is,
even today, acting as judge, jury, and executioner,

I might not be here now
telling you my life, my mythology,
as if it was just another bedtime story.

III.

Funny how we use the word "half" when we tell our stories.
To hurt we say, "half-human" "half-wit" "half-baked idea."

To heal we say, "my better half" "shared sorrow
is half the sorrow."

When he was a boy, my father was teased
about his height, called hating-tao,
or half a person, half-human.
Like Buan, my father became determined
to show them all, prove that
he was just as strong, brave, wise, whole.

When you were born, my friends said you were
hapa-haole, half-white and half-Asian,
a beautiful creation of two worlds,
two hearts coming together in love and family.
They may call you hapa, but you made me whole.

IV.

If you can't go home again,
then you must take home with you
wherever you go.

I call the Philippines home.
It's where I was born,
where I was given my first name,
where I learned how to say Mommy
and sing Nanay in the same breath.

I call America home.
It's where I claimed my true name,
where I found my true voice,
where I learned how to make my life, my heart,
and my songs light enough to carry.

My sister and I no longer live
in the same house, even the same state,
but wherever we can be together,
when we can be mothering sisters,
I feel like I have come home.

If home is where the heart is,
then wherever you two are,
I am home.

Oh, Mama

Sweets, are you crying?
It's okay. You can tell me.

What will we do when you and Daddy die, Mama?

You will forgive us our sins, as we forgive yours.
You will scatter our ashes over all you have inherited.
You will remember our stories, as we told them to you.
You will sing our songs to your children,
your grandchildren.
You will go on.

Just like Araw, Buan, and Tala.

Scatter the Ashes

Our father was dead.
Our mother was dead.
Our world was changed.

We had to scatter our father's ashes
over what was once the kingdom of Bathala.

At daybreak, Araw scattered Bathala's ashes over
the backs of eagles, agila soaring
above hills that are the color of cacao beans

the wide-brimmed hats of villagers
planting rice seedlings on terraced mountain fields

the opened sails of vinta
setting out across the open sea to fish and trade.

Tala sang to our father's ashes
and the ashes danced across the bridge
between day and night.

At nightfall, I scattered Bathala's ashes over
the lovers who meet at the riverbank
to steal a moment, a kiss

the dreamers who lie awake
and whisper questions to me in their hearts

the poets who sit upon the sand
to look out at the darkness into eternity.

The shining sun is my brother.
The brightest star is my sister.

I am the moon in the darkness
reflecting their light,
amplifying their songs,

guiding our people

on Earth as in Heaven.

We Belong

We are immigrants.
We get the job done.

We are exiles.
We build and rebuild lives where we must.

We are warriors.
We fight as if we will never die.

I.

I am too Pilipina for America.
I am too American for the Philippines.
I am too brown yet also too white.

My father gave me
too much fire.

My father set my heart afire
with the beauty of ordinary magic,
filling me with a passion for life.

Now I seek water
for I am thirsty
for questions,
for answers,
for experiences.

My mother gave me
not enough air.

My mother made my heart heavy
with fear, regret, disappointment, and
a longing for a safe place to call home.

Now I seek earth
that I may crawl away,
that I may stand my ground,

that I may walk with pride,
that I may run free.

If I am somehow both too much and not enough,
then maybe, maybe, I must be just right for me.
If I am just right for me, you can be just right for you.

II.

One mother made warriors by sending away
the lights of her heart.
The next mother made a warrior by beating
her fist against her heart.
This mother makes warriors by singing
the songs in her heart.

Every story I tell you is my story, anak.

My name is Buan.
My name is Elsie.

I am the goddess of the moon.
I am your mother.

You are my moonbeam.
You are my starshine.

They may call you hapa, but you are whole.
They may call you hapa, but you made me whole.

We are warriors.
We are goddesses.
We are lights.

We are mothers and sisters and daughters.
We are friends and family.
We are singers of stories.

We belong.

Mama, tell us another story

Let me sing you a song, sung by mothers since Dalisay.
A song about a star that twinkles between worlds,
the bridge between brother and sister,
between day and night, between light and dark.

Kislap, kislap bituin
Ano bang 'yong gawain

Sa ibabaw ng mundo
Parang hiyas na bato

Kislap, kislap bituin
Ano bang 'yong gawain

I have more stories to tell you.
Stories of longing and belonging,
of fighting and loving.

I will tell you another tomorrow.

For now, good night, my hearts.
Tulog na. Go to sleep.

Glossary

All gods and goddesses listed are from Tagalog mythology, from the island of Luzon in the northern Philippines.

Pronunciation Note: All vowels in Tagalog are short vowels. Each vowel indicates a separate syllable. So, the number of vowels in a word matches the number of syllables. If a syllable is capitalized, that is the syllable that should be stressed. If no syllables are capitalized, place equal stress on each.

adobo (ah-DOH-boh) – a Pilipino cooking technique, usually for pork or chicken, that involves a marinade of garlic, peppercorns, bay leaves, soy sauce, and vinegar

Agawang Sulok (ah-GAH-wang SUE-lohk) – a Pilipino game that is like a mix of tag and capture the flag

agila (ah-gee-LA) – eagle, may be derived from "águila," the Spanish word for eagle. The national bird of the Philippines is *Pithecophaga jefferyi,* also known as the monkey-eating eagle or great Philippine eagle.

Aman Sinaya (ah-MAN SI-nah-yah) – the Sea Goddess

"Amoy araw kayo." (ah-MOY AH-rauw KAH-yoh) – "You smell like the sun."

anak (ah-NAHK) – child, sometimes used like a term of endearment (i.e., "baby")

"Ang ganda nilang lahat, 'no?" (ang gahn-DAH nee-LANG LA-haht no) – "They're all beautiful, eh?"

Anitun Tabu (ah-nee-TUNE TA-boo) – the Storm Goddess

Araw/Apolaki (AH-rauw/ah-poh-lah-KEY) – the Sun God

araw (AH-rauw) – the sun

Ate (ah-TEH) – older sister or female cousin

"Ay sige na nga." (eye see-GEH nuh NG-a ["nga" is pronounced like if you said the word "singalong," but took away the "si" in the beginning and the "long" at the end]) – "All right, fine already."

bahaghari (bah-HUG-hah-ree) – rainbow

bahay kubo (bah-HIGH KU-boh) – a hut thatched with leaves from the nipa palm

bakit (BAH-kit) – why?

banig (bah-NIG) – a woven mat used for sitting (like for picnics) and sleeping

Bathala Maykapal (BAT-hah-lah MY-kah-puhl) – the Creator God

bibingka (bee-BING-kuh) – rice cake baked in a clay oven and served piping hot with coconut shavings. It is a traditional Christmas treat, eaten at breakfast or after Midnight Mass.

Bighari (BIG-hah-ree) – the Rainbow Goddess

bolo (BOH-loh) – sword-like machete that can also be used to cut down plants

Buan/Mayari (boo-AHN/MY-a-ree) – the Moon Goddess

buan (boo-AHN) – the moon

chismis (CHEES-mees) – gossip

"Cute mo naman."* (moh nah-MUN) – "Aren't you cute."

"Dahil Sa Iyo" (DAH-hill sah iYOH) – a popular Tagalog love song. The title means "Because of You."

Dalisay (doll-ee-SIGH) – the mortal mother of the celestial siblings

dalisay (doll-ee-SIGH) – pure, unblemished

Darna Komix – a series of comic books about a Pilipina superhero named Darna, created by writer Mars Ravelo and artist Nestor Redondo.

duyan (doo-YAHN) – cradle or hammock swing for a baby

"Galing!" (GAH-ling) – "Amazing!"

hapa (HAH-pah) – Hawaiian word for half that has been adopted by some Americans to refer to people who are "hapa-haole" or "half-white." "Hapa" by itself can also be used to refer to anyone who has mixed heritage comprising at least one Asian ethnicity and another/other ethnicity/ies.

hating-tao (HAH-ting TAH-oh) – half-human, half a person

Hoy! – Hey!

"Huwag po." (hoo-WAG poh) – "Please don't, [elder]." The word "po" is an honorific appended to sentences when you are speaking to someone older than you.

"*Immigration Passport* mo ito." (moh ee-TOH) – "This is your Immigration Passport."

isang kisapmata (ee-SUNG kee-SUP-mah-TAH) – one blink of an eye

"Isa pa!" (ee-SAH pah) – "One more!"

"Isa pa! *Tiebreaker* na 'to!" (nah toh) – "One more! This is the tiebreaker!"

Jack-en-poy – Pilipino name for rock-paper-scissors

"Kailangan *perfect.*" (kigh-LUNG-an) – "It must be perfect."

kalabaw (kah-lah-BOW, like "take a bow") – carabao or water buffalo

kamiseta (kah-mee-SHE-tah) – camisole or tank top

kapatid (kah-pah-TID) – sibling(s)

kare-kare (kah-REH kah-REH) – a Pilipino dish styled after Indonesian peanut curry; usually contains oxtail, eggplant, banana blossom, and string beans cooked in a creamy peanut sauce and served with rice

Kaunlaran (kah-UHN-lah-RUN) – Progress; the name of an elementary school in Makati City

Kidlat (kid-LOT) – the Lightning God

kidlat (kid-LOT) – lightning

kilos – kilograms

Kislap (kiss-LUP) – a popular supermarket tabloid in the Philippines. The Tagalog word "kislap" means "to twinkle."

kokak (KOH-kak) – the sound Pilipino frogs make.

"Kumusta?" (KUH-mus-tah) – "How are you?" Standard Tagalog greeting derived from "Cómo estás?" in Spanish.

Kuya (KOO-yah) – older brother or male cousin

Laban! (la-BUN) – Fight!

langka (lung-KAH) – jackfruit

lechón (leh-CHON) – roast pork, specifically an entire pig roasted on a spit over fiery coals

liwanag (lee-wah-NUG) – shiny light, as of a star

liwayway (lee-why-WHY) – dawn

Lola (LOH-lah) – Grandmother

lumpia (LOOM-pya) – deep-fried egg roll, made Pilipino-style with cooked ground pork and vegetables

"Mabigat ba iyan/'yan?" (ma-bee-GUT ba yun) – "Is that heavy?"

"Magpakabait ka, ha?"(mag-pa-KA-ba-EAT kah hah) – "Be a good girl/boy, okay?"

mahal ko (MA-hal koh) – my love

malong (MA-long) – long tubular cloth one-piece that can serve as a skirt or pants if girded at the loins

mayari (MY-a-ree) – owner

"May Yagit ba sa Amerika?" (my ya-GIT ba sa A-me-RI-ka) – "Is there [the TV show] Yagit in America?"

mestiza (mes-TEA-za) – a light-skinned Pilipina who most likely has mixed Spanish or American heritage

monggo guisado (mung-GOH gee-SA-doh) – mung beans cooked in pork broth (or boiled with pork bones), seasoned with garlic and onion, and garnished with bitter melon

na – already

Nanay (NAH-nigh) – Mother

Noche Buena (no-CHE bwe-na) – traditional Christmas Eve dinner, usually including lechón or roast pig. "Noche Buena" in Spanish means "Good Night" and refers to Christmas Eve.

para sa (pa-ra sa) – for

pasalubong (pa-SA-loo-bong) – souvenir gift

pastillas (pas-tee-yas) – milky, chewy candy made from condensed milk

pero (PE-ro) – but

peso (PE-soh) – Philippine currency

Pilipina – a Pilipino girl or woman

Pilipino or Filipino – the people of the Philippines. It has traditionally been spelled "Filipino" phonetically for English speakers, but Tagalog does not have the "f" sound, so Pilipinos are reclaiming the spelling to match the Tagalog pronunciation.

Pinoy/Pinay (pee-NOY/pee-NIGH) – slang shortcut for Pilipino/Pilipina

Pinoy pa rin (pee-NOY pa rin) – still Pinoy

puto bumbong (POO-toh boom-BONG) – purple rice cake baked in tubes. It is a traditional Christmas treat.

Salamat (sa-LA-mut) – Thank you

Santo Niño (SAN-to NEEN-yo) – Holy Child, Christ Child, most commonly used to refer to the statue of Jesus Christ depicted as a child

"Sarap!" (sa-rup) – "Delicious!"

Simbang Gabi (sim-BUNG ga-bee) – Midnight Mass

sinag (SEE-nug) – a beam or ray of light, as of the moon or sun. Mayari was strong enough to be a beam of sunlight, but she ultimately becomes goddess of the moon.

Sister/Sr. – "Sister" is the honorific for school nuns in the Catholic tradition; it goes before their first name. The abbreviation is "Sr." in the same way as "Mr." is the abbreviation for "Mister."

Tala (TA-lah) – the Star Goddess

tala – the morning star

"Tama na!" (ta-ma na) – "That's enough!"

Tatay (TA-tie) – Father

tikling (tik-ling) – cranes. Farmers in colonial Philippines built bamboo traps to catch the tikling and keep them from eating rice crops. The graceful way that the tikling avoided the traps inspired the Philippines' national dance of tinikling, in which dancers imitate the tikling birds stepping through the bamboo stick traps.

Tita (TEE-tah) – Aunt

Tito (TEE-toh) – Uncle

vinta (vin-tah) – a sailboat with multicolored sails unique to the Southern Philippines

yagit (ya-GIT) – rubbish or trash; can be used as an insult to describe a poor person

yaya (ya-ya) – nanny or caretaker, often also a housekeeper

Songs

Bahay Kubo

Bahay kubo, kahit munti
ang halaman doon ay sari-sari

Singkamas at talong, sigarilyas at mani
Sitaw, bataw, patani

Kundol, patola, upo't kalabasa
At saka meron pang labanos mustasa

Sibuyas, kamatis, bawang at luya
Sa paligid-ligid nito'y panay na linga

Nipa hut, even though it's small,
The plants that grow around it are varied:

Turnip & eggplant, winged bean & peanut,
String bean, hyacinth bean, lima bean.

Wax gourd, sponge gourd, white squash, pumpkin,
And there's also radish, mustard,

Onion, tomato, garlic, and ginger,
And all around are sesame seeds.

Twinkle, Twinkle Little Star

Kislap, kislap bituin
Ano bang 'yong gawain

Sa ibabaw ng mundo
Parang hiyas na bato

Kislap, kislap bituin
Ano bang 'yong gawain

Twinkle, twinkle little star
How I wonder what you are

Up above the world so high
Like a diamond in the sky

Twinkle, twinkle little star
How I wonder what you are

Afterword

Many of the stories Elsie tells in this book are stories from my life. Like Elsie, I was born in Manila, Philippines, and immigrated to America when I was nine years old. Ferdinand Marcos was the president of the Philippines for all my life at that point, and he was a dictator, presiding over one of the most brutal regimes the Philippines has ever known. My parents decided to leave our homeland after a man named Benigno "Ninoy" Aquino, Jr., was assassinated for leading the resistance movement against Marcos.

Ninoy's assassination ushered in a time of political unrest and my parents feared we would be in danger. It is true that Pilipinos who wanted to immigrate to America, Canada, or other countries had to enter a visa lottery. Usually, people would get one chance at the lottery, but my parents got called a second time due to a clerical error in their favor. We moved to America in April 1984. Marcos was ousted in 1986 after the People Power Revolution.

Like Elsie, I was also an outspoken young lady who briefly lost her voice and name on the way to my new home. Like Elsie, I learned how to speak up, claim my name, trust my voice. Like Elsie, I felt like an outsider for most of my life and only started to feel like I belonged anywhere after I had my two daughters. As in the poem "We Belong," people may call my daughters hapa, but they made me whole.

Speaking of the word *hapa,* I want to acknowledge that it is often a controversial term. It is originally a Hawaiian word meaning "half," and some people believe that it should only be used to refer to people who are half-Hawaiian. In the Pacific Northwest where I live, however, the word *hapa* has become part of our cultural vernacular; people are comfortable using it to refer to those who are half-Asian and half some other ethnicity. It was my Hawaiian friends who first called my own children "hapa."

Lastly, I want to note how important songs are in the book. I included the entirety of "Bahay Kubo," a Tagalog folk song describing the bounty of the land, because it was how I learned the names of many vegetables. Like many tribal societies, Pilipinos passed on their stories and their knowledge of the earth to their children through song.

Poetry is music, poems are songs, and so I wrote this story in poems to pass on my story, Elsie's story, Buan Mayari's story, through song. Thank you for reading.

Maraming Salamat

This book would have stayed locked away in my heart forever if not for the support and (sometimes tough) love of my friends and family of choice and chance.

Thank you, Margaret Stohl, for being my mentor, mamacita, and friend. You are the first person to tell me I should be the first person to take myself seriously. I am forever grateful to you for making me cry during our first lunch at Araya, when you asked why on earth I'm not writing this book. You lit a fire under me that day, mama, and here we are. So! What's next?

Thank you to my superstar agent, Sarah Burnes, for your mad hustle on my behalf. I am so thankful for you, my cheerleader, draft editor, and co-conspirator during the publishing process. You've got Big Auntie Energy and I feel so blessed you are on my team.

Thank you to my editor and publisher, Lauri Hornik, for helping me make my voice stronger and clearer. I appreciate how open, flexible, and supportive you were throughout the revision process for this book.

Thank you to my amazing beta readers—Karinn Figdore, Stacey Janssen, Grant Mackay, Elisa Mader, Fritzie Mercado, Betsy Ptak, Randy Ribay, Jonathan To, Amy Tsai, Julie Uyeda, and Ling Yeh—and the Neurotic Fortitude Club, especially Christine Feraday, Grant Roberts, Jill Scharr, Mallory Schleif, and Christine Thompson, as well as the Wonder Woman Wednesday Writers. Not only did y'all help me make beta betta, you also listened to my ramblings and/or sat with me under my desk until I pulled myself together so I could write. Your devoted friendship and relentless cheerleading humbles and fortifies me.

Thank you to my stellar youth beta readers, including Ellie and Noah Tsai, Kaiden Uyeda, and Nadiya and Kalani Yeh-Koth. All of you asked the most difficult— and therefore most helpful—questions while reading my early drafts and you inspired me to make the story clearer and brighter for readers like you.

Thank you to my Hiponia family for everything. Daddy, I miss you every day, and I hope I have made you proud. Mom, thank you for helping to make me the

woman I am. Kuya, we may have fought as fiercely as Araw and Buan, but we also love as fiercely. Maricel, thank you for being my first best friend, rival, teacher, and partner-in-crime. You will forever be my baby. Heartcha always.

Thank you, Dusty, for loving me for nearly half my life. The family we made, as well as the family we have chosen, sustains and enriches me. I love you.

Most of all, thank you, Diana and Tala, for inspiring me to write this book for you. You two have taught me to ask better questions and seek truer answers. I love you two so much and I am so lucky to be your mama. Our world is brighter and warmer because of both of you.